THE COLLAPSE OF ILLUSIONS

L C Singh

Published by : Disha Publication
ISBN: 9789371868778

Printed and bound in India.

Dedicated

To my father-
who carried the burden of others,
and smiled

Contents

Introduction

Sometimes, everything looks
fine on the outside—
you show up, do your work,
care for people—but inside,
something keeps nudging you.

A quiet feeling that something isn't right.
You start asking:
What is this all for?
Where is this race heading?

Desires begin to feel more real than you.
Stress, anxiety, and fear
become part of your every day.
People you love drift away.
Sometimes, you're asked
to let go of what you hold dearest.

And slowly, you begin to wonder.
Who am I without all this puzzle?
What's right, what's wrong?
Is there a God? And if there is...
where is He?

You pray, but the anxiety doesn't leave.
You keep going,
scrolling, smiling, performing,
but nothing seems to settle you.
If you've felt this way,
this book is for you.

We call it The Collapse of Illusions—
because that's what begins when life quietly
asks you to stop, and see what's real.

Not in some loud, dramatic way.
But in the small, honest moments
when you start noticing what you've
always accepted without question.
When you stop pointing outward, and
begin to ask, "how did all this get built?"

This isn't a book of answers.
It won't tell you who to become.
But it may help you notice the quiet
structures—ideas, emotions, and
identities—that quietly shape how we live.
They weren't always ours.
They were passed down,
picked up, put in place.

And over time, they became us.

But when we begin to see them,
really see them, something shifts.
This is not about becoming more.
It's about letting go of what isn't true.

If you've made it this far,
you're already on the path.

And if you're ready to see differently,
to shift how you perceive reality,
go on. Turn the page.

Preface

The Collapse of Illusions

It started long ago, under the open sky.

As a child, I would lie still and look up
at the stars, at the dark that held them.
The village around me would go quiet, but
the sky never did. It hummed. A soundless
music, almost blissful. I didn't know
what it meant.
But I felt it.

And then the questions began.

Why am I here?
Do I matter?
If I were to disappear... would the world
still go on... or would it vanish with me?

I didn't speak these questions aloud.
I just carried them. Like a secret
hum beneath my skin.

That wonder never left me.
Through school, work, success and loss.
Through every applause and every silence.
I kept watching. And feeling. And asking.

This book is part of that lifelong inquiry.
Not into ideas, but into presence.
Not to find grand truths, but to gently
uncover what lies beneath the noise...
identity, fear, time, love...
and the illusions we live by.

I offer it as it came to me.
Through moments, not methods.
Through observation, not instruction.
You may find thoughts here that unsettle
you, calm you, or simply stay with you.

If they do, let them.
Somewhere, the night sky is still watching.
And maybe, just maybe, it remembers too.

— L.C.

Note to the Reader

This book does not challenge any faith.
It does not aim to disprove, discredit,
or replace what you believe.

It simply observes life—through systems,
entropy, and awareness.
Not through mythology.
Not through commandments.

If belief brings you peace, let it be.
But if you've ever wondered
what remains when belief fades,
this book is written for you.

The Blink That Stayed

It didn't begin with light
or consciousness.
It began with chemistry.
On a planet still forming—violent,
scorched, soaked in storms—
something improbable happened.

Earth then was not Earth as we know it.
No green, no blue, no breath.
Only molten rock, volcanic clouds,
oceans of acid, and gases like methane,
hydrogen cyanide, ammonia—toxic,
unstable, reactive.

And somewhere within this chaos,
a fragile reaction began.

Maybe it was lightning
that struck a tidepool.
Maybe it was heat rising
from deep-sea vents.
Maybe clay beds trapped
just the right mix of molecules.

We don't know exactly how.
But something triggered a sequence.
Not a spark, but a loop.
A loop that didn't stop.

The Unlikelihood of Life
We call it abiogenesis.
Life arising from non-life.

But the word hides the absurdity
of its own claim.

Because for a self-replicating molecule
to form, the odds are estimated
at one in $10^{40,000}$— a number so vast,
it practically means never.

The Improbable Equation

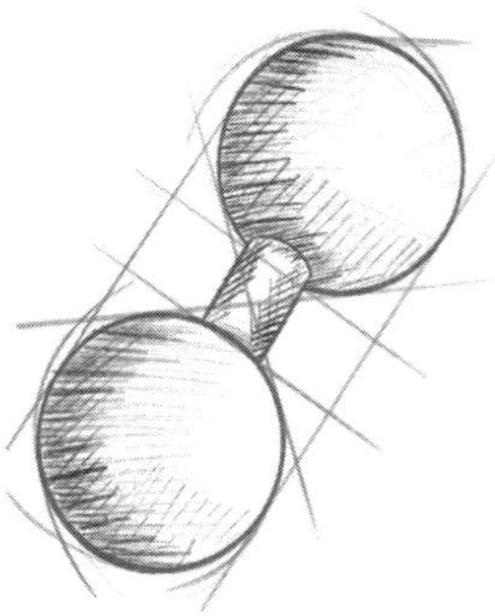

The probability of abiogenesis, the spontaneous formation of a self-replicating molecule under prebiotic conditions, is estimated at 1 in $10^{40,000}$.

For context:

- *There are ~10^{80} atoms in the observable universe*
- *And only ~10^{43} Planck time intervals have passed since the Big Bang*

The odds border on the impossible.
Yet... it happened. Once. Here.

Molecules do react all the time.
But they don't organize themselves,
protect themselves,
or loop their own instruction set,
unless every condition is aligned:

- Liquid water, to dissolve and carry
- Reactive gases, to donate and bond
- Heat and UV, to energize
- No free oxygen, because it would have destroyed the fragile reactions
- A catalytic surface like clay or metal
- And above all: Time. Not hours. Not days. Millions of years.

Each of these alone is common.
Together, they form a chemical window
narrower than belief.

And yet, through that window,
something slipped in.

Why It Should Have Died

That first formation of life had
no nervous system, no immune response,
no error correction, no membrane.

It should have unraveled in seconds.

The seas were unstable.
The sun, unfiltered by atmosphere,
rained radiation.
Molecules collided, scattered, broke.

But one loop.
Just one
held on long enough
to make a copy.

And then, another.
And again.

Not with perfection.
Not with purpose.
But with enough rhythm
to survive its own instability.

The Paradox

This is where logic begins to strain.

Replication is not chemically necessary.
Rocks don't replicate.
Flames spread, but they do not preserve.
Even reactive molecules
don't repeat unless forced.

So why did this loop persist?

It had no will.
No plan.
No concept of death or future.

Yet it behaved as if something mattered.
As if ending wasn't an option.

This is not yet consciousness.
It's not even instinct.

But it is movement in a direction.

Not Because It Could, But Because It Did

The standard explanation is simple:
it survived because it could.

But that's not an answer.
That's a description.

This loop did something strange:
it acted like it feared vanishing,
without knowing fear.

It endured, without being aware that
it was enduring.

And from that quiet resistance,
evolution began.

The Blink That Stayed

No one knows how many attempts
were made. To replicate. To stay.
To echo themselves just once more.

Maybe billions. Maybe trillions.
Tiny loops of chemistry assembling by
chance, then vanishing without a trace.

Some couldn't hold.
Some didn't copy in time.
Some simply dissolved.

But one.
Just one
persisted.

It looped with just enough stability.
It copied just early enough.
It adapted just fast enough.

And from that moment,
life had momentum.

Not soul.
Not design.
Just refusal.
And that refusal echoed
through oceans, through time,
through single cells, fish, apes, and us.

It was not a voice.
It was not a command.
It was a vibration—
a memory,
a tendency,
a tremor that did not dissolve.

We are not here because we are special.
We are here because
one blink refused to vanish.
And now, it watches through our eyes.

The Illusion of Intention

The blink stayed.
But it had no eyes.
No memory.
No knowing.

So why did it persist?

That question hovers
over the birth of life.
We say life wants to survive.
But the first life had no want.
No self. No sense. No fear.

It was a fragile loop.
Barely stable.
Yet it acted
as if ending was something to resist.

Why?

What gave lifeless matter
the impulse to endure?

Not Just a Reaction

Replication is not required by physics.
It is not inevitable.
Molecules react, bind, break apart.
They do not repeat themselves.
They do not anticipate.

The earliest living system,
if we dare call it that, had no strategy.

No immune response.
No repair mechanism.
No organelles.
No senses.
No boundary.

And yet, it replicated.
Not once. Not perfectly. But enough.

Enough to matter.

It's not that it knew what to do—
but it behaved as if something
needed to continue.

A loop turned into momentum.
Not because it chose—
but because it kept going.

And that was enough
to begin the illusion.

The Illusion of Intention
Intention Is Not Required

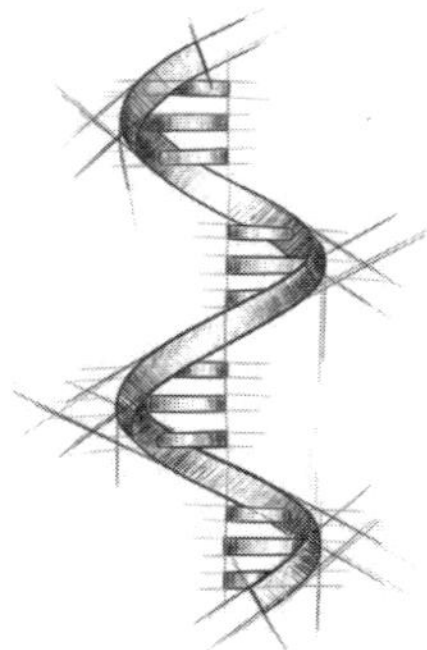

*The earliest molecular replicators,
likely strands of RNA or pre-RNA,
exhibited self-reinforcing chemical stability.*

*This behavior is not driven by intention,
but by thermodynamic favorability
and local energetic coherence.*

*In closed systems, entropy increases.
But in open systems with energy input
(like early Earth), temporary pockets
of order can emerge.*

*Replication, once triggered,
becomes a kinetic pathway—not a choice,
but a chain reaction that sustains itself.*

*It mimics purpose. But it is only a reaction
pathway with persistence bias.*

*The illusion of "intention" is an artifact
of this self-sustaining behavior.*

Every theory
of life's continuation begins here.
And every one carries
a hidden contradiction.

Let's walk through them.

1. The Mechanical View:
"It Survived Because It Could"

This view says: once replication happened,
it continued.
No mystery. Just possibility fulfilled.

But that explains nothing.
Why copy at all?

Rocks exist. They don't replicate.
Fire spreads. But it doesn't remember.

Replication is not chemistry. It's behavior.
A pattern that preserves itself.

And that implies direction,
even if no one is steering.

It's not that the molecule chose,
but the result mimics choice.
And that imitation of intention
has fooled us ever since.

2. The Entropy Argument: "Life Serves Decay"

Some physicists argue life isn't
a miracle at all.
It's a more efficient way to spread entropy.

Living systems take in organized energy
(sunlight, glucose) and break it into lower
forms: heat, waste, disorder.

Life, in this view, is a tool for the universe
to accelerate its own unraveling.
But if entropy is inevitable,
why create complexity to achieve it?

Why create systems that resist ending?
Why replicate at all?

And why feel?

Why evolve a species that fears death,
writes poetry, and questions its own
beginning?

This theory explains life's cost,
but not its motive.
It says life breaks things down.
But it doesn't explain
why something tried to hold.

3. The Selfish Gene: "Replication is the Point"

Dawkins gave us the metaphor
of the selfish gene.
Genes behave as if they want to be copied.
Life, he said,
is just the gene's survival machine.

It's clever.
But it's backward.

Because there were
no genes in the beginning.

No DNA.
No chromosomes.
No machinery.
Just a few molecules forming a loop.

What was selfish in that moment?

The metaphor inserts
intention by implication.
It borrows language from feeling
to describe what never felt.

It works for evolution.
But not for origin.

What They All Miss

These theories describe
how life behaves once it begins.
They explain the behaviour.

But not its birth.
They describe survival.
But not the impulse to survive.

They explain what stayed.
Not why it stayed.

They treat that first moment
as if it needed no reason.
But in doing so, they miss the rupture.

Because in a universe
where most things fall apart,
this one didn't.

And that's not chemistry.
That's coherence.

A Different Direction

Let's look at it differently.
No gods. No purpose. No metaphor.
Just a field.

A field of vibration.
Oscillation. Tension. Return.
In this field, everything,
light, matter, memory,
is just frequency.

Most frequencies cancel.
Some fade.

But once in a while,
one finds balance.
It persists. It aligns.
It stays.

Maybe life wasn't a thing.

Maybe it was a pattern that didn't collapse.

A tremor that looped just right.

It didn't mean to stay.
But it did.
And that's how illusion was born.

The illusion that something
wanted to exist.
The Tremor That Stirred the Field

Perhaps the first movement
was not survival.

But the residue of a tremor
that had nowhere to go.

It wasn't instinct.
It wasn't awareness.

But it was a movement
in the direction of being.

Something continued.
Something resisted vanishing.
And from that,
the rhythm of replication was born.

Not because it should have.
Not because it knew.
But because it was aligned with the field.

And the field let it stay.

What Comes Next

Maybe it wasn't just chemistry
that endured.

Maybe it was a subtler vibration that held,
a frequency that slipped
through in silence, a loop that became
more than its molecules.

And from that loop
came the first pulse.

A movement that noticed
it had moved.
And that was life before it knew its name.

The First Pulse

Author's Reflection

Some of what you're about to read
may seem abstract, even mystical.
But it rests gently on the shoulders
of science, just not the parts
we've fully understood yet.

Physics today doesn't describe reality
as solid objects, but as fields of vibration.
String theory imagines everything—matter,
energy, even gravity—as ripples across
deeper dimensions. Some interpretations of
consciousness now suggest it may not arise
from the brain alone, but may be seeded in
the very fabric of existence.

This chapter isn't a theory.
It's a reflection on what may have moved
first. And what that movement might
still be whispering to us.

Before time, before space, before even
separation, there was just a field.

Not of matter, not of form, just vibrations.
A field alive in motion, yet still.

A single continuity,
with no edges, no direction.
And within it, something stirred.

A cluster of frequencies—a configuration—
became aware, powered
by the intentionality to be.
It didn't see or hear anything. It just was.
It had no language, yet somehow it knew:
"I am."
And suddenly it realised;
it was no longer the field,
And a sensation arose:
"I may not remain."

That was the first tremor.
The earliest whisper of fear.

Not fear of death as we know it,
but a primitive, raw tension.
A shift in harmony. A disturbance in flow.
Not an event, just a recognition:
Something around me is not me.

From that instant,
the field was no longer seamless.
A line, faint but real, had been drawn.

And with it came sensing.
Crude, scattered, and instinctive.
Heat, friction and imbalance.

These weren't receptors; not yet.
They were reflexes curling back inward,

A recoil from now; a sensation of outside;
as the field began to know itself as self.

This fragile awareness, born of tension
and fear, triggered the next act: replication.
Not to multiply, but to persist.
Because now, there was something to lose.

But replication didn't erase the original.
Each copy was still the whole.
Each split carried the same pulse,
the same memory, the same awareness.

Some flickered out quickly.
Some held on.
But then something unexpected:
What one encountered, all remembered.
No delay, no storing; just transmission.

This was no random evolution.
It was a living improvisation.

Each extinction became a learning.
Each insight a quiet correction.
Each survival, a signal to adapt.

The field was learning without knowing.
And that led to mutation—not over time,
but almost instantly.
A collective self sculpting
itself through feedback.

The field, once still,
was now alive with intent.
Not personal intent.
Just the will to remain.
The earliest shape of form,
drawn from the need to see itself apart.
To shift. To stay alive.

The oneness was now in motion.
Still whole; but quivering with tension,
preference, direction.

The story of individuality had just begun.

The Mirror That Forgot

In the beginning, there was no form.
Only a field of possibility—silent,
undisturbed, unexpressed.

It wasn't emptiness.
It was Nihilence.
The presence without identity.
A stillness that simply was.

Around it lay a latent layer of potentiality.
Not energy. Not matter.
Just the readiness to become.

Then came a ripple.
A movement within awareness itself.
Not of thought, not of intent,
but of awareness touching its own edge.

And in that instant,
potentiality collapsed into motion.
Energy was born;
not as a thing, but as a becoming drawn
from the silence of the field.

But awareness didn't stop.
It turned inward, forming
instruments within itself
to know what it had become.

It created vision, so it could perceive light.
It created touch, so it could feel edges.

It created thought,
to trace what wasn't there.
Emotion, to weigh the invisible.

With each new sensory system added,
perception created a new reality.
With each layer, something formless
was shaped—into time, space,
direction, and form.

But then, a new turn.

As these instruments refined, a new
identity began to crystallize:
The self. The "I". The one who experiences.

At first, it was soft, fluid, curious.
But slowly, it grew stronger.
Firmer. Defined.

And with that, something was lost.

The direct communion, the silent knowing,
the ability to feel the other as oneself—
began to fade.
Communication now needed signals.
Sounds. Gestures. Words.
And even those fell short.

The more precise the identity,
the greater the separation.

Yet the urge to reconnect never left.
A trace of the original unity
lingered like a scent.
A whisper: You are not alone.

And so, we began to create.

The telephone—a wire across silence.
The car—to collapse space.
The internet—to speak without waiting.
Music—to feel without translation.
Social media—a mirror,
desperate to be seen and echoed.

Every breakthrough that excites us,
does so for one reason:
It promises to make us whole again,
even if only for a moment.

The thrill is not in speed or power.
It's in the illusion of reunion... the wall
between self and other thinning,
even if only for a moment.

But before we move forward,
we must pause.

To see not just the separation of identity,
but the fragility of the very material,
that made identity possible.

What took shape—bones, breath, skin,
synapse—was never eternal.
It was never meant to be.
The structure, no matter how refined,
was built with elements
borrowed from the field itself.
And to the field, they must return.
Erosion, corrosion, aging,
and decay—these are not failures.
They are the natural signature
of the form dissolving
back into the formless.
The body, like a sandcastle at low tide,
slowly releases its shape.

And this erosion has a name.
We call it age.

Not just the passage of time,
but the cost of holding separation.
The toll exacted by form.

Time is not simply a clock.
It is the consequence of becoming distinct;
Of being bound by structure.
Of existing apart.
And this sense of time
brings with it a deeper anxiety—
a fear not just of change,
but of disappearance.
And so begins the next turn.

A more complex emotion.
Fear.

Not the primal reflex of survival,
but quiet hum beneath identity.
The fear of not existing,
the fear of losing control,
the fear of the other.

This fear becomes language.
It becomes memory.
It becomes strategy, defence, ego, war.

And to manage it,
we begin to play a new game.

The grand game of EcoSpace.

A game where distance is power.
Where boundaries define meaning.
Where separation becomes architecture.
Where the world becomes divided.
Not just by land or thought,
but by the illusions we create to feel safe.

The Architecture of Fear
and the Grand Game of Space

Before fear, there was peace.

Not the peace of silence or stillness,
but the peace of wholeness.
No separation, no comparison, no loss.

Then came form.
Then came the self.
And with it,
the space between forms and self.

Space began as sanctuary.

A corner to rest.
A place to belong.
Food, shelter, family, privacy.
Room to breathe, to be, to grow.

This was sacred space—not a possession,
but a condition for life.

But slowly, something shifted.

The need became a want.
The want became a pursuit.
And the pursuit became a defense.

A car. A larger house. A sense of status.
Comfort for the self. Comfort for the child.

Air conditioning. Insurance. Surveillance.
Fat bank balances. Bigger boundaries.

And then, greed.

More of everything.
Not just to live, but to win.

More influence. More attention.
More space than others.
Not to feel safe.
But to feel superior.

The primitive mind returned.
Territorial, insecure, competitive.
The self, began hoarding space.
Not to survive,
but to protect its illusion of worth.

And thus began the quiet illness.

Not of the body,
but of the being.

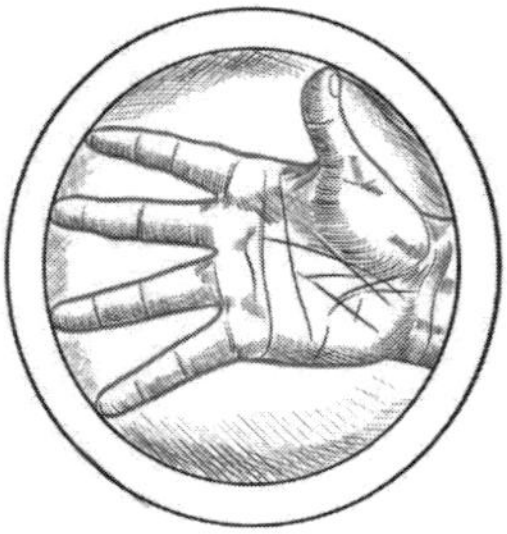

The psyche, bloated with wanting,
began to fracture.

Wrath replaced presence.
Addiction replaced meaning.
Comparison replaced connection.
Control replaced compassion.

We became bigger, and emptier.

Consumed. Confused. Inhuman.
Not because we turned evil,
but because we were afraid.

Fear did not arrive as a monster.
It arrived as a whisper:
"What if I lose what I have?"
"What if someone else takes it?"

And to guard against this whisper,
we built walls.

Mental. Emotional. Relational.
We called it ambition.
We called it pride.
We called it success.

But it was always fear,
disguised as space.

The Emotional Descent

This fear didn't explode overnight.
It arrived one emotion at a time:

First came stress,
a tightening around effort.
Then disappointment,
when the effort didn't yield.
Then comparison,
when others seemed ahead.
Then envy, then jealousy,
then fear of losing.

That fear turned inward.
We grew pensive. Withdrawn. Guarded.
Then came anger—lashing out to defend
what felt at risk.

Each of these widened the emotional gap.
Each one deepened the distance,
between self and other,
between now and meaning.

And with that widening,
something began to leak.

The Birth of EchoTime

Even a whisper of emotion...
delight, doubt, hurt...
traces the shift in our invisible space.

A compliment opens it up,
softening the edges of the self.
A mild critique draws it inward,
like a flinch.

We live in a breathing field around the 'I'.
Swelling or shrinking with every word
we hear, every glance we catch.

The felt space around the self shrinks
with threat, expands with acceptance.
It shapes our emotions by altering
how safe we feel to exist.

Our emotions are not reactions.
They're echoes of how much space
we feel allowed to exist in.

Not all time is equal.
Physical time moves by the clock—
minutes, days, years.
It ages the body, drives seasons,
ticks forward no matter what.

But there is another kind of time.
Invisible. Psychological. Perceptual.
We call it EchoTime.

EchoTime is not how long you live.
It's how deeply you feel what you live.

- A single moment of shock,
  feels like a lifetime.
- An afternoon in love,
  gone like a breath.
- One betrayal echoes for decades.
- A moment of peace, last forever.

Imagine an inner hourglass.
Physical time flows at a constant rate.
But EchoTime flows through an orifice
shaped by emotions.

- In love, it narrows.
- In presence, it pauses.
- In trauma, it bursts wide open.
- In grief, it floods.
- In longing, it loops.

You don't age just because of clock time.

You age faster because of how
much EchoTime you've spent.

Every unresolved moment—grief, betrayal,
regret, humiliation—replays inside
the mind like it's still happening.
And the body doesn't know the difference.

Each replay triggers the release
of stress hormones: cortisol,
adrenaline, norepinephrine.

These chemicals prepare the body
for danger—racing heart, tense muscles,
shallow breath.

Useful in a real emergency.
But when EchoTime traps us
in emotional residue, the body stays
on alert. Not for minutes,
but for months, even years.

This is what accelerates aging.

Chronic stress shrinks brain regions
like the hippocampus, weakens
the immune system, disrupts sleep,
and increases inflammation.

Cells fray faster.
EchoTime becomes
a biological debt paid silently.

How EchoTime Alters the Body

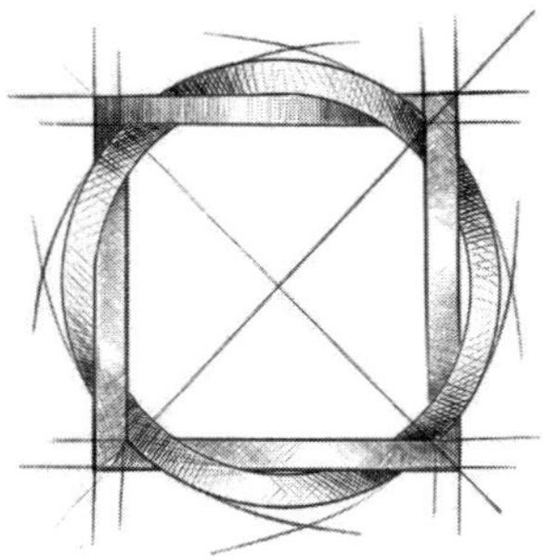

- *Trauma → cortisol + adrenaline → accelerated aging*
- *Love → oxytocin + dopamine → cellular repair*

EchoTime isn't abstract.
It speaks to the body through chemistry.

Your biology listens not just to time,
but to how you experience it.

But the same mechanism can nourish us.
When we feel peace, love, awe,
connection—the body responds
with another set of chemicals.
Oxytocin. Dopamine. Serotonin.
Endorphins.

These aren't just pleasant feelings,
they are regenerative signals.
They slow down cellular decay.
They whisper: you are safe,
you are loved, you are not alone.

This is why two people of the same age
can look, and feel, decades apart.

Not because one lived longer,
but because one carried
more unresolved time.

The Two Great Leaks

The greatest losses of EchoTime
don't come from losses.

They come from shock.

- Sudden death of a loved one.
- Abandonment without closure.
- A future lost in an instant.
- Betrayal by the one you trusted most.

These events burn EchoTime.
Not once, but again and again.

The mind replays what it cannot resolve.
And every replay spends more.

But not every moment drains.
Some give back.

- Sitting with a loved one in silence.
- Holding someone while they cry.
- Laughing with old friends.
- A quiet walk through trees.
- The breath between notes in music.
- The presence of a cat in your lap.

These moments don't burn EchoTime.
They hold it.
They seal the breach.

That's why hours feel like seconds
when you're in love.

And seconds feel like years
when you're alone, afraid, or grieving.

When Echo Time Runs Out

So what happens when EchoTime is gone?

The body may still be alive.
The calendar may show
more years to come.

But the self feels... finished.

Two outcomes often appear.

1. The Blocked Mind — The Psychopath

Some minds, overwhelmed by EchoTime
cost, shut the valve completely.
They stop feeling.
Not as a choice, but as a defense.

They block memory. Seal emotion.
They become cold, functional, strategic.

There is no empathy.
Not because they are monsters,
but because there is no Echo left to spend.
Others become data.
Life becomes calculation.
Connection becomes risk.

This is not power.
It is survival, without aliveness.

2. The Exhausted Mind — The Numb

Others keep feeling...
until there's nothing left.
They bleed EchoTime
until the vessel is dry.

What remains is not sadness.
It is numbness.
No will to move.

No strength to hope.
No desire to protect or create or connect.
They are not angry. Not cruel.
They are just… done.
And this is perhaps even harder to see.

Time and EchoTime: A Subtle Dance

Physical time and EchoTime
don't intersect.
But they influence each other
through bio-interjection.

- Physical pain triggers emotional states—leaking EchoTime.
- Emotional depletion alters brain chemistry—accelerating aging, weakening immunity.

Your back may break from an accident.
That's physical time.

But your emotional collapse
after the accident?
That's EchoTime leaking.

They are separate timelines.
But their feedback loop is
what we call suffering.

The Real Crisis

We check for breath.
We check for heartbeat.

But we forget to check for EchoTime.

This is the epidemic beneath all others:

- Burnout is not overwork.
  It's EchoTime depletion.
- Addiction is not pleasure-seeking.
  It's time-looping.
- Narcissism is not confidence.
  It's emotional bankruptcy.
- Indifference is not strength. It's the silence that comes when Echo runs dry.

The Only Restoration

There is no therapy more effective
than presence.
There is no medicine more potent
than love.
There is no wealth more protective
than meaning.

These don't just feel good.
They seal the leak.

They stop the unnecessary expenditure.
They rebuild the hourglass.

To sit with someone without agenda.
To return to nature.
To breathe without performing.
To cry without shame.
To be without trying.
To listen without judgement.

These are not luxuries.
They are resets.

You don't have to be enlightened.
You don't have to be healed.
You don't have to be wise.

You just have to stop draining.

And then, life begins again.

The Tribe and the Disappearing Self

Once fear found a home in the individual,
it began searching for company.

And so, we built tribes.

Not of kin, but of kind.
Not of love, but of likeness.

People who looked like us, prayed like us,
spoke the same language,
ate the same food.
We came together to feel less alone,
but ended up feeling more divided.

This wasn't connection.
It was camouflage.

We traded empathy for allegiance.
We replaced understanding with identity.
We no longer asked, "What do you feel?"
We asked, "Which side are you on?"

Borders. Religions. Flags. Creeds.
Each a costume for fear
pretending to be pride.
Each a line drawn in the sand,
to keep the other out,
and keep the illusion in.
And so the self, once whole,
fragmented further.

Now it wasn't just I versus you.
It was us versus them.
We belonged to groups,
but not to ourselves.

We surrendered awareness to ideology,
curiosity to conformity,
kindness to command.

And the fear got stronger.

Not because the threat grew,
but because we stopped
questioning the game.

Every tribe promised safety.
But what it delivered was control.

- Speak like us or be shunned.
- Agree with us or be cancelled.
- Die for us—and you'll be remembered.

These were not invitations to truth.
They were instructions to forget.

Forget who you were before the story.
Forget the stillness before the side.
Forget the echo of your own breath,
and replace it with the roar of belonging.

And in that roar, the being was swallowed.
Not by evil.
But by the hunger to matter.

The Great Inversion

Once, you had a self.
And joined a group.
Now, you have a group.
And search for the self.

This is the inversion.

We no longer explore truth.
We inherit it, weaponized
and pre-approved.

We no longer belong to the earth.
We belong to a flag, a market segment,
an algorithm.

We no longer look for meaning.
We look for alignment.
And what we find is exhaustion.

Because no tribe is big enough
to hold your entire being.
And no ideology is pure enough
to replace your intuition.

So we chant. We post. We march.
We convince others.
Not because we're sure,
but because we're scared.

And yet, beneath all of it,
something in us remembers.
The warm silence before the labels.
The shared breath before the border.
The childlike smile before the tribe.

That memory is the key.

Not to undo the world,
but to remember the self within it.

Because every being came here
for something true.
And no system, no label, no tribe
can offer that truth.

Only you can.
And only when the fear of being alone
is smaller than the joy of being whole.

The Maze of Fear

But remembering is not easy.

Because fear is not just a feeling.
It is a map.

And the mind, once afraid,
begins to follow it blindly.

The reptilian brain, our oldest layer,
seeks one thing: safety.
It doesn't dream. It doesn't feel.
It doesn't care.
It protects.

Then comes the emotional brain,
which craves EchoSpace.

A space to be felt, to be held, to be real.

Even the slightest shift in emotion—
joy, hurt, irritation—
follows a quiet movement in space.

A compliment lands gently:
"You look radiant today,"
and something opens.
A subtle softening around the self.

A passing critique,
"Maybe not your best color,"
and the space draws inward.
Like breath pulled tight.

It isn't the words alone,
but what they do to our standing.
The invisible field around the 'I',
stretching or shrinking
with every glance,
every tone,
every moment of being seen.

Our emotions are not reactions.
They are responses
to how much space
we feel we have
to simply exist.

And beneath that lies the being,
the still point at the center,
which asks for just one thing:
freedom to be.

But in chasing safety,
we often sacrifice echo.
And in seeking echo,
we forget freedom.

We begin with good intent.
To secure, to protect, to belong.
But soon,
we find ourselves in a maze.

A maze built by fear,
mapped by memory,
lit by the flicker of pride and pain.

We act inside this maze,
possessed by fear and all its dialects:
ambition, jealousy, comparison,
even love twisted into need.

And the more we try to escape,
the more entangled we become.

Because the maze
was never meant to lead out.
It was designed to keep us circling.

The more you prove, the less you feel.
The more you fight, the more you forget
what you were fighting for.

What began as a survival instinct
becomes an identity.
What began as protection
becomes performance.

What began as a journey
becomes a prison.
And we don't even see it.
Because the maze is not made of walls.
It is made of thought.

Only if we could see the maze...

Only then would we stop running.
Only then would we hear the echo
of our true voice.
Only then would we remember—
we were free before we were safe.

Entropy, Disturbance, and the Feedback Loop of Life

Every system—
biological, emotional, social—
is built to maintain balance.

Whether it's your nervous system,
your family,
or the global economy,
each one absorbs input, adjusts,
and returns to equilibrium.

But every action,
especially emotional action,
creates disturbance.

And that disturbance doesn't vanish.
It travels through the system
and returns to you.

Not as punishment.
Not as morality.
But as a cybernetic consequence.

Cause and Effect, Rewired

When you act from anger,
fear, manipulation,
or even silent resentment,
you're not just expressing an emotion.

You're introducing entropy
into a system.

You shift the emotional atmosphere.
You inject instability.
You change the state of others.
And the system begins to react.

This reaction is not personal.
It is systemic logic:
What disturbs the whole
must be addressed,
one way or another.

The Three-Level Loop

Disturbance flows
through three distinct levels:

First—
System Response.
Immediate or delayed outcomes...
rewards, exclusions, resistance,
praise, retaliation.
They reshape your environment,
and your place within it.

Second—
EchoSpace Disruption.
Emotional distance expands.

Trust weakens.
Resonance disappears.
You begin to "lose people"
without knowing why.

Third—
EchoTime Leakage.
The mind replays
what the heart couldn't settle.
Each replay consumes your energy,
your attention,
and your lifespan.

Finally,
all of it flows back into the body.

Fatigue.
Insomnia.
Illness.

Sometimes breakdown,
sometimes burnout.

You feel it as stress—
but it is really the system's whisper:
"You have unsettled your own world."
When the System Strikes Back

But not all responses
are subtle or delayed.

When the disturbance becomes too large,
when your presence
threatens the coherence
of the system itself,
the response may turn direct
and physical.

You may become a target,
not because of your identity,
but because of your impact.

You may be removed,
rejected, terminated.

Not by an individual,
but by the system's invisible hand
moving through its agents.

A whistleblower loses their job.
A truth-teller is silenced.
A rebel is eliminated.
A hyper-reactive employee is benched.

Sometimes, even your
biological system joins the defense.
You fall sick.
Your immune system weakens.
Your body stops protecting you,
because you've become a source of noise,
internally and externally.

These are not random events.
They are entropic
rebalancing responses.
You disturbed the field,
so the field responded.

The Feedback Loop of Emotional Entropy

The System Echo Cycle

1. You act →
2. Your action disturbs or aligns a system →
3. The system responds with reward
or disruption →
4. That response alters your emotional state →
5. Which reshapes your EchoTime →
6. Which affects your next action

This loop is continuous, cybernetic, and real.

It is how the future is formed.

Emotion → EchoSpace →
System Disturbance →
System Response →
EchoTime → Body →
Future Behavior

This loop defines not just your past,
but the trajectory of your future.

It explains why
your relationships shift.
Why your health fluctuates.
Why you sometimes feel punished
without cause.

Because what you do
inside the system,
and what you carry
in your emotions,
is never without consequence.

Even silence is an input.
Even inaction is a signal.

The System Remembers

You may forget
what you did or felt.
But the system doesn't.

It logs everything.
It responds to energy,
not just action.

To presence,
not just performance.

And these systems
are not limited to your personal world.

They scale.

The family is a system.
So is a nation.
So is a species.
So is the planet.

Every one of them runs
on thresholds and tolerances.
Every one of them holds—
until it breaks.

Entropy builds silently—
until the balance collapses.

Economies crash.
Trust evaporates.
Ecosystems fail.

The same feedback loop
that governs your body
governs the world you live in.
Every action
is a release of energy.

Every release
either integrates
or fragments the system.

Fragmentation is entropy.
And entropy is the true cost.

This is the third entropy block.

Not time.
Not memory.
But disturbance.
What you do matters.
Not morally,
but mechanically.

And the system,
at every level,
remembers.

The only way to restore balance
is not through control—
but through coherence.

To bring
your action,
emotion,
and intention
into alignment.

This is not morality.
It is mechanics.

And once you see it clearly,
you don't need fear to guide you.

You only need awareness.

The Unpredictable Field and the Influence Beyond Logic

You can map emotion.
You can track echo.
You can chart system response.
But there is always something
left outside the circle.

A presence.
A force.
A nudge that shifts the outcome,
even when all variables seem known.

We call it chance.
We call it fate.
We call it the universe.

But it is neither divine nor random.
It is simply the unmeasurable influence
of the field of potentiality.

The Field

Beyond the self, the system,
and the echo there is a field.
Not of things, but of tendencies.

It holds possibilities, not certainties.

It is what determines
why two people do the same act—

but one transforms,
and the other breaks.

It is what explains
why healing happens suddenly,
why accidents feel fated,
why some moments feel orchestrated
by something larger.

Not a script.
But a bias in the field, a gentle push.

This field is not predictable.
But it is influenced.

Influence Without Force

The field is shaped by:

- Presence
- Purity of intent
- Depth of awareness
- Unforced love

These qualities don't cause outcomes.
But they align you
with what is trying to emerge.

Just like a sail doesn't create wind—
but catches it.
Just like still water reflects the stars.

You cannot command the field.
You can only become permeable to it.

And when you are...

Surprising clarity arrives.
Undeserved grace appears.
Patterns shift without logic.

The Three Pillars — Final System Snapshot

Pillar (Bottom): Physical Time
- *Governs: Body, decay, aging*
- *Leaks Through: Entropy*
- *Balanced By: Rest, repair*

Pillar (Side): EchoTime
- *Governs: Emotions, perception*
- *Leaks Through: Trauma*
- *Balanced By: Love, awareness*

Pillar (Upper): Systemic Action
- *Governs: Collective behavior*
- *Leaks Through: Disruption*
- *Balanced By: Alignment, truth*

The Final Loop

So the full Life Theory
is not a closed circuit.
It ends with a permeable membrane—
a crescent, open at one end,
receiving influence
from the unknowable.

This is why life is never formulaic.
Why systems fail.
Why transformation is real.

Because in the end,
you are not just a being inside a system.

You are also a receptor in a field.

And that field...
sometimes answers without being asked.

The Answer That Doesn't Speak

Sometimes, you find yourself moving
without will,
without strategy,
without knowing
why the next step feels inevitable.

You leave something behind,
not because it broke,
but because something else began to stir.
You arrive somewhere unfamiliar—
but feel at home in the uncertainty.
You speak a word,
and only later realise it was not yours.

And then, you shudder.

Not from fear.
But from the strange recognition
that you were being moved,
gently, precisely,
by something that does not speak in words
but places you where
the answer might be seen.

Not heard.
Not explained.
Just felt.
That is the field.

It doesn't solve.
It surrounds.
It doesn't intervene.
It allows.

And when your inner question
has ripened—

it doesn't give you a reply.
It gives you a moment.

And that moment...
becomes the answer.

The Field Responds to Pure Intentionality

The field does not speak language.
It reads resonance.

It does not respond to thoughts.
It responds to alignment.

When you stop trying to control.
When your desire is quiet but whole.
When your question is honest enough
to dissolve the self, the field responds.

Not by giving you what you want,
but by placing you where you need to be.

It is not obedience.
It is coherence.

This is not belief.
This is what remains...
when all noise falls away,
and only the pulse of being remains.

True Prayer

True prayer is not a request.
It is not made of words.
It is not directed to someone.

It is a state of inner coherence,
where your being aligns with your
longing—not as noise, but as stillness.

You become transparent to the field.
And the field,
without voice,
without shape—responds.

Not always with outcome.
But always with presence.

This is not worship.
This is oneness without identity.
When you no longer separate
yourself from what you seek—
you no longer need to ask.

Because the answer
has already begun to move through you.

All True Insight Is Prayer

The greatest physicists,
philosophers,
and thinkers don't discover
truth by force.
They tune themselves to it.

They question with depth.
They listen with silence.
And at a certain point,
they are no longer the thinker.
They become the instrument.

And when the field is ready,
it speaks.

Through equation.
Through metaphor.
Through knowing without knowing why.

This is not belief.
This is resonance.
And it is as close to prayer
as any mind can go.

Final Passage: Life Theory

The Return to Silence

What begins must end.
Life is limited.
But existence has no end.

Nihilence.
Neither born, nor dying—
is the stillness beneath becoming.

The field of potentiality arises,
disappears,
and returns again.
Not to repeat,
but to reveal.

I came to be.
I wandered.
I dissolved.
I will continue.
Not in direction,
but in spontaneity.

There is nothing to solve.
Nothing to hold.
Only the movement that remains
when meaning dissolves into presence.
Since Nihilence is eternal,
existence is eternal.

There is no reason for emotion.
No urgency in stillness.
Just being.
Just moving.

And in this,
all things are already complete.

We came from the Complete.
We were born complete.
We got lost to learn, evolve, and be
complete again.

To return to the Complete...the Nihilence.

The Collapse of Illusions

For centuries,
humanity has searched
for an external truth.
A divine force,
a moral code,
a guiding purpose.

But when we strip away the illusions,
when we look not through belief,
but through understanding—
we see:

Life is not governed by gods
Nor by moral absolutes.

It is governed
by physical limits,
by emotional echoes,
and by the entropy of our actions.

The Three Pillars of Existence:
Physical Time, EchoTime, and Action

Our lives are not infinite.
They are controlled by three forces.

The first:
The Physical Body and Time
We exist within biological constraints.
The body deteriorates.

The cells follow their programmed limit.
And at around 150 years,
no matter what we do,
life reaches its upper boundary.

The second:
EchoTime
The mind does not experience time
as the clock does.
It stretches.
It contracts.

Trauma widens the orifice.
EchoTime drains.
Love and presence seal the opening.
EchoTime is preserved.

Mental health depends
on how wisely EchoTime is spent.

The third:
Action and Systemic Entropy
We live inside systems.
Family, society, law,
nation, Earth, the universe.

Every action
creates entropy.

It disturbs the system.
The system reacts.
Sometimes gently,
sometimes not.

Everything we experience...
joy, suffering, morality,
even our sense of self,
is just the interplay of these three forces.

The Universe as the Master System

But we are not just part
of human-made systems.

We exist within
larger, living ones,
governed by the same rules.

The Earth has its own tolerance.
When we push it too far,
it responds...
climate,
disasters,
collapse.

The solar system,
the galaxies...
they influence us,
down to our rhythms,
our sleep,
our tides,
the space-time we breathe in.

Even the universe...
it too follows entropy.

It expands toward its limit,
toward collapse, or reset.
The same way a person breaks,
a civilization can fall.
A planet too
has an entropic breaking point.

We are inside of inside of
endless hierarchy of systemic
entropy exchanges.
From the individual to the cosmic.

The Death of the God Debate

And this is where
the illusion of God collapses.

For thousands of years,
we've asked:
Does God exist?
What is right and wrong?
What is the purpose of life?

But when we understand
that all of existence
is governed by systemic limitations,
these questions dissolve.

God was an explanation
for what we didn't understand.

Now, we see laws of entropy,
time, and feedback.
And they explain everything.
Morality is not absolute.
It is how systems self-regulate.

"Right" and "wrong"
are not divine.
They are shifting balances...
of energy,
of survival.

Purpose is an illusion.
What exists
is how we move through the system...
consciously
or unconsciously.

The search for God ends...
because there was never a God to find.
Only constraints to understand.

The Final Realization:

The Game of Life is Entropic Balance

So what is left?
What is truth,
if not religion,

philosophy,
or morality?

Truth is simple.

Existence is not divine.
It is entropic.

Time is not measured.
It is felt.

Morality is not universal.
It is a response.

There is no cosmic plan...
only energy moving through systems.

And when we see this clearly...
we are no longer lost.

We don't need belief.
We need understanding.

We don't need purpose.
We need awareness.

Before we disappear

The five dissolutions:

We spend our lives circling around
five questions. Never fully seeing them,
never fully escaping them.
Identity. Death. Love. Time. Creation.
They shape everything we are.
And quietly... they dissolve.

Identity

What you call *yourself* is not real
in the way you think.
It is an echo, assembled from memory,
sensation, reaction, and the stories you've
been told. Identity is layered within
EchoTime, the lingering impression
of every emotional moment.
The 'I' is simply what survives
the noise of experience.

But identity is not fixed, it is a reflection
on moving water. And like all reflections,
it depends entirely on the surface,
the angle, and the light. What you hold
so tightly is already dissolving, constantly
reshaped by perception.

To believe in a solid identity
is to live in illusion.
To see through it is not death.
It is liberation.

Death

We fear death because we believe
it ends something essential.
But what ends is form.
What fades is memory.
What dies is only what was never
permanent to begin with.

Death is not the opposite of life.
It is part of the cycle of appearance
and disappearance.
It does not interrupt awareness.
It interrupts continuity.

What remains,
when the senses fail,
when the story ends,
is the same awareness
that was always there.
You do not disappear.
You return.

Love

The potential for love is born
from separation.
Without separation, there is no longing.
And without longing,
there is no bridge to build.

Fear creates the distance,
empathy begins to cross it.
Empathy is what allows awareness
in one form to resonate with another.
It is the soft undoing of fear.

And in that undoing, love arises,
not as an emotion, but as recognition.
A reunion with something
you never truly lost.

Love is not the opposite of aloneness.
It is the proof that we were
never truly alone.

Time

There is no time.
Not in the way we perceive it.
Time is the echo of change,
stitched together by memory.
Space is the context in which
this echo stretches.
Before time and space,
there is only pure awareness.
Not moving. Not still. Just aware.

We call it void, but it is not empty.
We call it silence, but it is not absent.
It is simply *present.*

Nihilence is not a vacuum—
it is presence before perception.
And when awareness becomes
aware of itself, intentionality arises.
With it, the illusion of a beginning.

There was no creation.
Only appearance. And disappearance.

Creation

Nihilence is pure awareness—
aware of itself.
It is not a being, not a void, not a god.
It does not observe. It simply 'is'. And yet,
within that stillness, something stirred.

The awareness turned intentional.
Not through thought, but through
the sheer force of *wanting to be.*
That was the first movement.
The origin.

Intentionality did not create time and
space. It generated the field of potentiality.
From this field, everything emerged.
Not by design, not by chance,
but by inevitability.
Life was the first form
that could hold awareness.

Nihilence took form in that moment.
Not as a creator, but as presence
inhabiting form.
The cosmos, then, is not a creation.
It is an appearance.
And life is not an accident.
It is awareness expressing itself.

The intensity of that first intent—
so absolute—
must have released infinite energy.
Enough to give birth to stars,
gravity, matter, and time.

That energy, formless yet overflowing,
is what many traditions have called
Shakti. Not mythology, but the name
for energy before identity.
The pulse of existence,
waiting in stillness, activated by intent.

This is the architecture behind what we see.
Not divine. Not random.

Simply inevitable,
once awareness became intentional.

So the world is, because you are here.
When you are not, there is no world.
But the light that saw it all remains,
without a name, without a need to return.

The Blink and the Gentle Exit

I was the Intentionality.
Not born. Just... stirred.
Not to become. Only to be.

I was the blink.
And the blink created its own world.
Time unfolded, forms arose,
and I entered.
As thought, as breath, as I.

I chased permanence,
clung to echoes,
took illusions to be real.

At times, I heard the whisper...
to transcend the illusion,
to find the truth...
but I was lost in the maze.

As the absurdity of fear melts,
and ripples begin to settle,
I do not need answers.
I do not need form.

Even the “I” begins to fade.
The dance is complete.

No gates.
No judgment.
Just a gentle return to the field.

To Nihilence.
Not an end,
but a soft dissolving.

Because the world was never outside me.
It emerged with me.
And with my exit,
it disappears.
Quietly.

There was never anything to lose.
Nothing to hold.
Only the play.
The Lila.
The cosmic dance of creation.

Epilogue

Some illusions collapse in an instant.
Others take their time.
But once seen, they can't be unseen.

This book wasn't written to impress,
explain, or persuade.
It was written to hold a mirror—
and then quietly step aside.
The truths here aren't absolute.
They're simply a window.
A chance to pause, peep, and explore.
No conclusions,
just enough to think and reflect.

What you do with that is yours.

If something stirred—an old thought,
a forgotten feeling, a quiet recognition—
attend to it.

You don't need to become more.
You just have to be enough.

There is a presence that remains
when the noise fades.
It doesn't chase.
It doesn't explain.

It simply is.